D0548187

This book
belongs to:

_____

MESSAGE TO PARENTS

This book is perfect for parents and children to read aloud together. First read the story to your child. When you read it again run your finger under each line, stopping at each picture for your child to "read." Help your child to work out the picture. If your child makes a mistake, be encouraging as you say the right word. Point out the written word beneath each picture in the margin on the page. Soon your child will be "reading" aloud with you, and at the same time learning the symbols that stand for words.

EDITED BY
DEBORAH SHINE

DESIGN BY
CANARD DESIGN, INC.

Copyright © 1988 Checkerboard Press, a division of Macmillan, Inc.
All rights reserved.

CHECKERBOARD PRESS, and their respective logos
are trademarks of Macmillan, Inc.

The Gingerbread Boy

A *Let's Learn to Read* Book

Retold by Debby Slier

Illustrated by Jill Dubin

Brown Watson

ENGLAND

man

woman

house

wood

children

There was once a little old

and a little old who lived in a

little beside a big . They

were very happy except for

one thing – they had no .

One day, when the little old

was baking gingerbread

biscuits, she had a small piece

of dough left over.

"I will make a gingerbread

," she said. So she rolled

out the dough and cut it in the

shape of a little 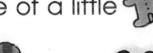. She gave

him candy , and candy

 on his braces. Then she

popped him into the oven to

bake.

boy

two

eyes

buttons

boy

woman

door

door

woods

When the gingerbread was ready, the little old opened the oven . But before she could lift him, the gingerbread jumped right out of the oven and ran out the kitchen , down the path, out the garden gate, and into the .

The little old ran after him. As she ran she called, "Stop!

Stop!" But the gingerbread

just laughed and said:

"*Run, run, as fast as you can,*

You can't catch me,

I'm the gingerbread man!"

man

woman

The little old was working in

his garden, and when he saw

the little old chasing the

gingerbread 🍪, he decided

to help.

"Stop! Stop!" shouted the little

old 👤. But the gingerbread

boy just laughed and called:

"Run, run, as fast as you can,

You can't catch me,

I'm the gingerbread man!"

The little old 👤 and the little

old 👩 couldn't catch the

gingerbread 🍪.

boy

On and on ran the gingerbread , across a field. Soon he

met a .

"Stop! Stop!" said the .

"I want to eat you!" But the

gingerbread just laughed

and called:

"Run, run, as fast as you can,

You can't catch me,

I'm the gingerbread man!

I ran from the old ,

boy

cow

man

and I ran from the old ,

And I can run away from you,

I can, I can!"

woman

cow

boy

horse

rn

The ran after the gingerbread , but she couldn't catch him.

On and on ran the gingerbread until he came to a beside a .

"Stop! Stop!" called the .

"I want to eat you!" But the

gingerbread just laughed

and ran on.

woman

man

cow

horse

boy

"Run, run, as fast as you can,

You can't catch me, I'm the

gingerbread man!

I ran from the old ,

and I ran from the old ,

I ran from the ,

And I can run away from you,

I can, I can!"

The ran after the

gingerbread , but he

couldn't catch him.

The gingerbread ran on

and on until he came to a .

He could not swim across, for he

would get soggy and fall to

pieces at once. He did not know

what to do. Just then a

came by.

river

fox

boy

fox

woman

man

cow

horse

"Here, jump on my tail, gingerbread , and I will take you across the river," said the

"You will be safe from the old , the old , the , and the ."

So the gingerbread boy

jumped on the  's tail, and

the jumped into the river.

As the swam across the

 he said to the gingerbread

, "Hop on my back,

because you may get wet if

you ride on my tail."

river

boy

fox

river

nose

The gingerbread moved onto the 's back.

When they were in the middle of the , the said, "The water is very deep here. I am afraid you will get wet. Sit on my ." So the gingerbread moved onto the fox's .

Suddenly the  threw back

his head, and SNIP-SNAP went

his teeth. He ate the

gingerbread  in one big

bite! And that is exactly what

gingerbread s are made for

– to be eaten!